THANKS TO THE SUN

By : Vinny Green

**G-SQUARE PUBLISHING
YOUTH DIVISION
G-SQUARE-PUB@OPTIMUM.NET**

All G-Square Youth Publications are inspired by the G-Square Division of

"Young Minds Inspiring Our Time."

**These works are Kid Tested
&
Youth Reviewed**

Dedicated to the Young Minds of Our Time

G-SQUARE KINGS AND QUEENS

Within all G-Square Youth Publishing works, Our Young Minds will find words colored in purple, a color representing the royalty of each of our growing young minds.

For each budding King or Queen who sends G-Square the meanings of those purple words, a certificate recognizing their efforts will be sent to them, acknowledging the growth in their vocabulary and **self-esteem**.

Send definitions to:
G-Square-pub@optimum.net

All purple words must be defined in order to be recognized as a "G-Square Youth, Budding Young Mind."

THANKS TO THE SUN

Have you ever looked upon the Sun, thought about from where its beauty comes?

Have you ever wonder how the sun came to be; was it shaped like clay or heavenly words spoken so that humans may live and breathe?

Is the Sun just a big top, spun for fun, and as the days run and run, playing with the Sun is just not as much fun.

Is the Sun set to run and run and run, or does it lose energy, grow dim, and cease to be the Sun?

Does The Good Lord spin again or just let it drop, moving on to some other galactic top?

Is it all a *cosmic* game, by some unknown name, that is played until it becomes crazy and *lame*?

If we can play games, why can't the Good Lord do the same?

Have you ever stopped to thank the Sun for rising in the sweet times, as well as when there are none?

Have you ever paused to *acknowledge* the Sun for the work it has done, for no other reason than it is the Sun?

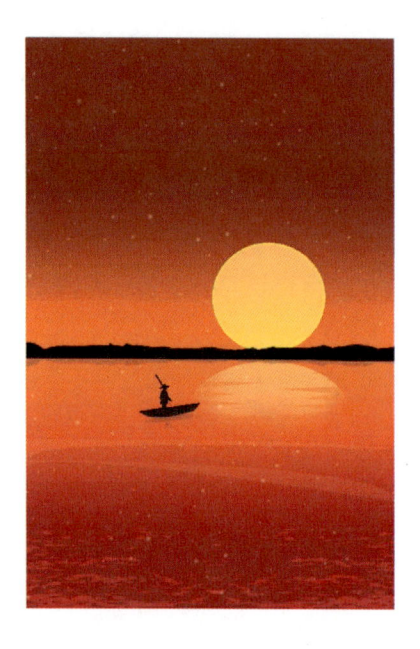

Have you taken the time to understand that you exist because the Sun has risen, again and again, at a time and place *prescribed* by God?

Remember, there is no need to plant a seed without asking the Sun to meet the needs of that seed.

All the things that we deem great; would be no more, if the Sun did collapse and *disintegrate*.

We all think we are so cool as if we actually had a hand in creating this godly plan.

Why not start this day with a glance to the sky and give sincere thanks to the one on high for shaping the Sun and allowing it to run and run and run.

ABOUT THE AUTHOR

Vinny Green is the Chief Executive Officer of G-Square Publishing. He is married with four children and four grandchildren whom he loves unconditionally.

Like the Sun, it is Vinny's greatest wish to also be able to meet the needs of his children and grandchildren and that they grow up to be well-known contributors to society.

Vinny has spent much of his adult life combating crime and teaching in several universities, colleges, and, when needed, other countries.

Thanks to the Sun, is Vinny's second book into the genre of children's stories. He has also written books in other genres but he has great joy in writing children's books. He and his Youth Editor and niece, Jaila Marie McCoy, are intent on traveling the nation, and if need be, the world, in sharing their books and trying to help children whenever they can.

YOUTH EDITOR

Hi, everyone, my name is Jaila Marie McCoy, and I am in the 7th grade. I live in Elizabeth City, North Carolina. Since I was six years old, I have been helping my Uncle Vinny edit his children's books and one or two of his adult novels. It has been a great experience.

I could not believe it when I actually saw my suggested changes appear in his books. I was even more blown away when Uncle Vinny allowed me to partner with him in the book called, My Hat, please buy it when it comes out.

At first, I thought being an author would be boring, but now that I have actually experienced it, I have changed my whole outlook on writing books and doing Youth Reviews.

Now I think being an author is really fun because you can start from nothing and end with a whole new world with just a keyboard and an idea.

When I grow up, I don't know exactly what I will end up being, but one thing I do know is that I will be famous! So maybe one day you might be purchasing one of my books, and don't worry, I will make sure to include my favorite Uncle.

I hope you enjoyed reading the book "Thanks to the Sun." When Uncle Vinny gave it to me for review, he said that he thought that it might be good for a ten or eleven-year-old. After reading the book and enjoying it, I felt that it would be better for an eight or nine-year-old.

Until I reviewed this book, I never gave much thought about the sun except that I love being in my backyard or on the beach enjoying the rays of the sun. Until I read this book, saying, thank you, to the sun was never on my mind. Time to fix that, so, thank you sun for all that you do, and thank you, God, for giving us such an awesome gift.

I'm going to share this book with everyone that I know and even some people that I do not know. That's my job as the "Youth Reviewer."

I am hoping that Uncle Vinny and I can continue to write books together and make my friends and other kids smile and recognized how blessed we are by gifts from above, like the Sun.

Oh, and make sure you go and check out some of our other children's books or some of Uncle Vinny's adult books! This is Jaila Marie McCoy, and this is my Youth Review.

G-Square Publishing
888c 8th Avenue, NY, NY 10019
Suite 424

Made in the USA
Columbia, SC
19 November 2021